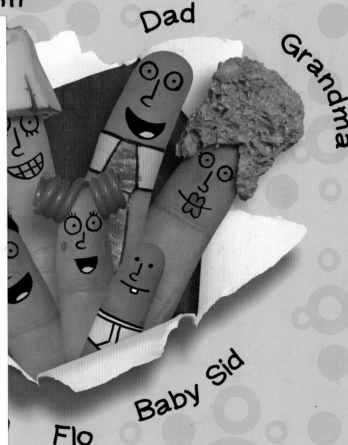

Mum

Dad

Grandma

Baby Sid

Flo

This book is dedicated to
Akira, Arthur, Ella, Finn and Iris

EGMONT
We bring stories to life

First published in Great Britain in 2014
by Egmont UK Limited
The Yellow Building, 1 Nicholas Road, London W11 4AN
www.egmont.co.uk

Text and illustrations copyright © David Sinden, Nikalas Catlow, Matthew Morgan 2014

The moral rights of the authors and illustrators have been asserted.

ISBN 978 1 4052 7174 5

A CIP catalogue record for this book is available from the British Library.

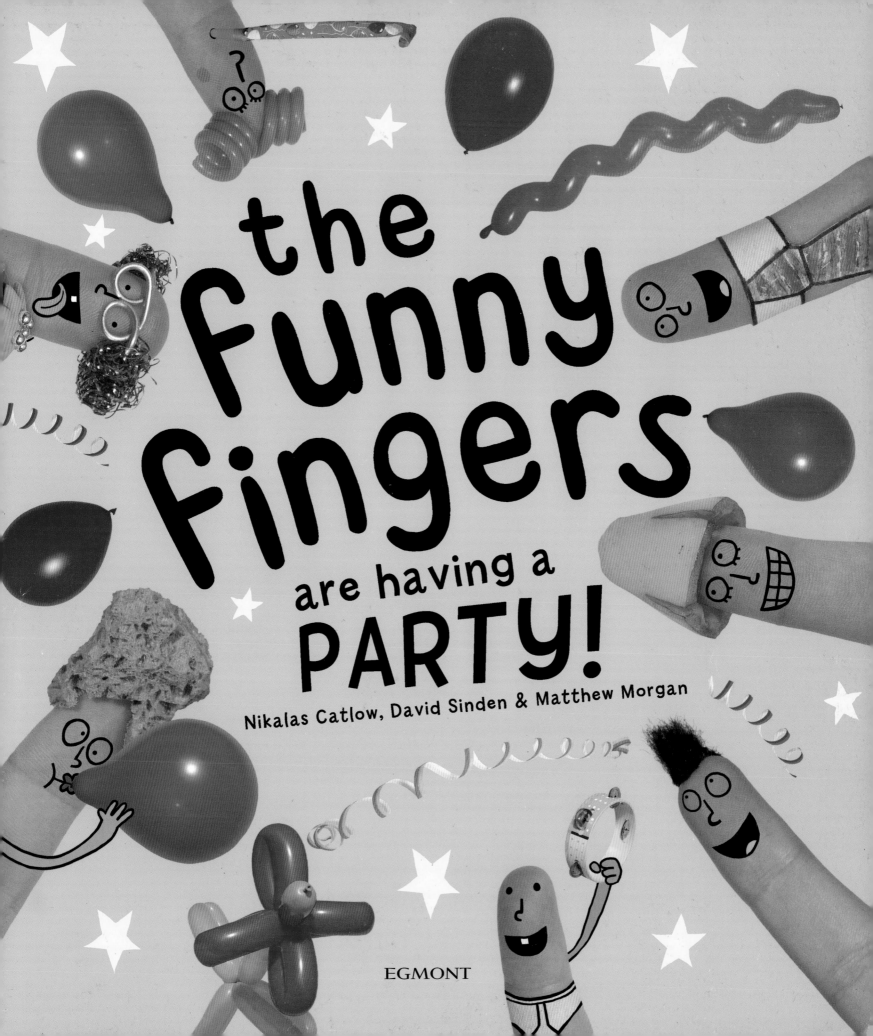

The Funny Fingers were an unusual family but
a very happy one. They loved to have fun . . .

. . . and nothing was more fun than a party!

"Whoopee! Let's have a party tomorrow!" said Flo.
"We can invite all our neighbours!"

The Funny Fingers glued, glittered and stickered
some fabulous party invitations to send out.

The Funny Fingers' neighbours were very pleased to be invited to a party . . .

The Rosy Toes brought flowers.

The Sticky Fingers brought cakes.

And the Fancy Fingers brought presents.

Mrs Toe leaned out of her window and screeched: "Stop that party at once!"

But everyone was having too much fun to hear.

Finn and Flo were face painting with their friends.

"I'm a butterfly!" fluttered Flo.

"And I'm a tiger," growled Finn.

Mum and Dad were balancing party hats and juggling creamy cakes.

Grandpa, Grandma and the Rosy Toes were playing with balloons.

And Baby Sid and the rest of the party guests were having fun on a bouncy castle.

"Wahey!"

"Woo-hoo!"

"Mmmm!"

The Terrible Toes were furious that no one was listening to them.

"WE SAID, STOP!" shouted Mr Toe. "STOP HAVING FUN!"

Errol, the Toes' pet foot monster, peered curiously over the hedge. He'd never seen a party before.

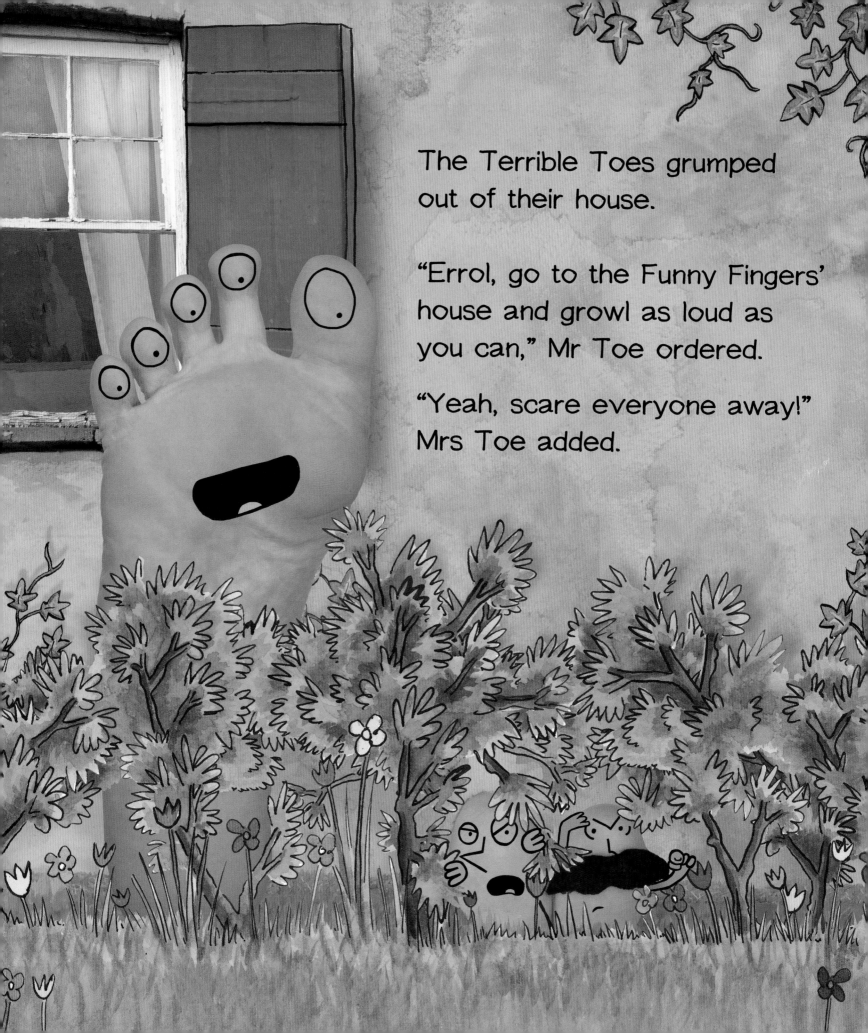

The Terrible Toes grumped out of their house.

"Errol, go to the Funny Fingers' house and growl as loud as you can," Mr Toe ordered.

"Yeah, scare everyone away!" Mrs Toe added.

At the Funny Fingers' party, everyone was dancing in the fizzy drink fountain.

Grandpa was spinning on his head when Errol burst in.

"Uh-oh! A foot monster!"

But when Errol heard the music, he forgot all about growling and started dancing too!

"Hey, Errol's come to join in!" Flo said.

Errol seemed to like parties, especially gobbling up the party food . . .

. . . and playing party games.

BOING!

"Hey, Errol, let's play Hide-and-Seek next," said Finn.
"Close your eyes, count to ten and then come and find us."

"Psst, Finn," Flo whispered from her hiding place.
"Look, Mr and Mrs Toe are coming to play too."

But the Terrible Toes hadn't come to play, they'd come to check that Errol had scared everyone away.

"Incredible! The house is empty," Mrs Toe said. "Errol has actually done as he was told."

"Good pet, Errol,
you big oaf," said Mr Toe.

Errol hopped to the living room. He appeared to be looking for something.

"Good idea, Errol, make sure there's no one left," Mr Toe said.

Errol went to look upstairs.

"Nope, no one in here," Mrs Toe said.

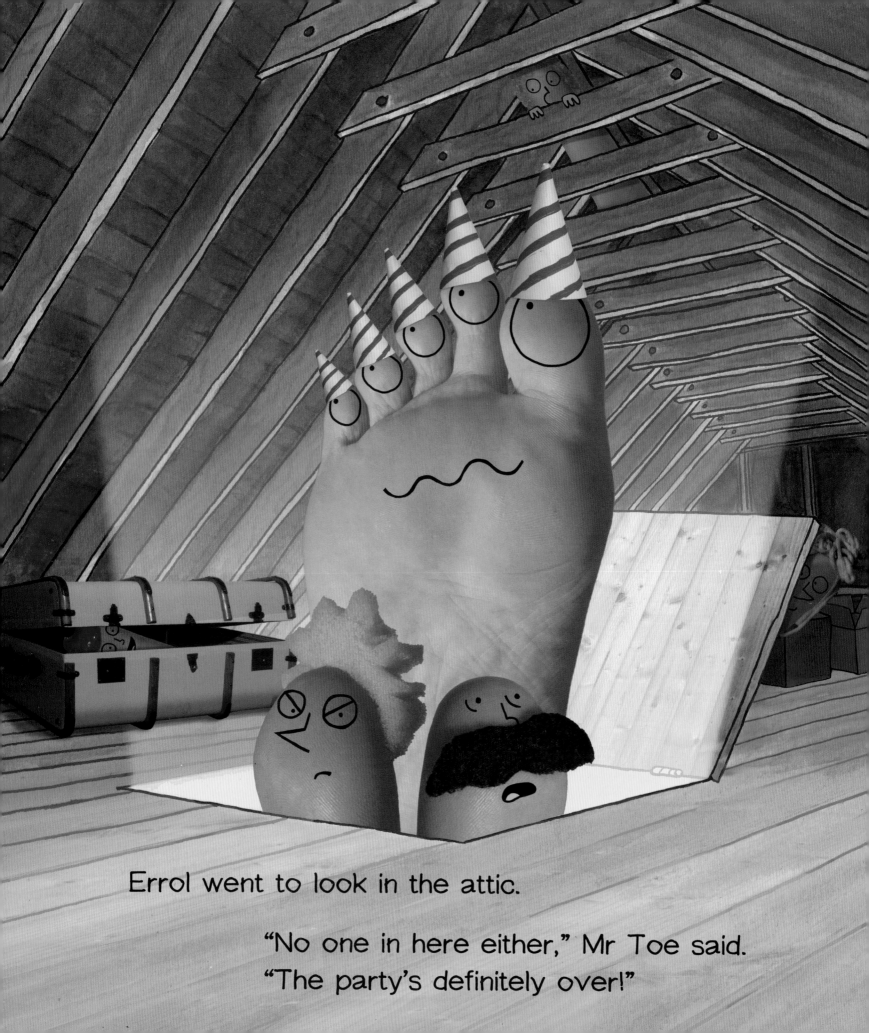

Errol went to look in the attic.

"No one in here either," Mr Toe said.
"The party's definitely over!"

But on their way out, the Toes suddenly heard a giggle from underneath the kitchen table . . .

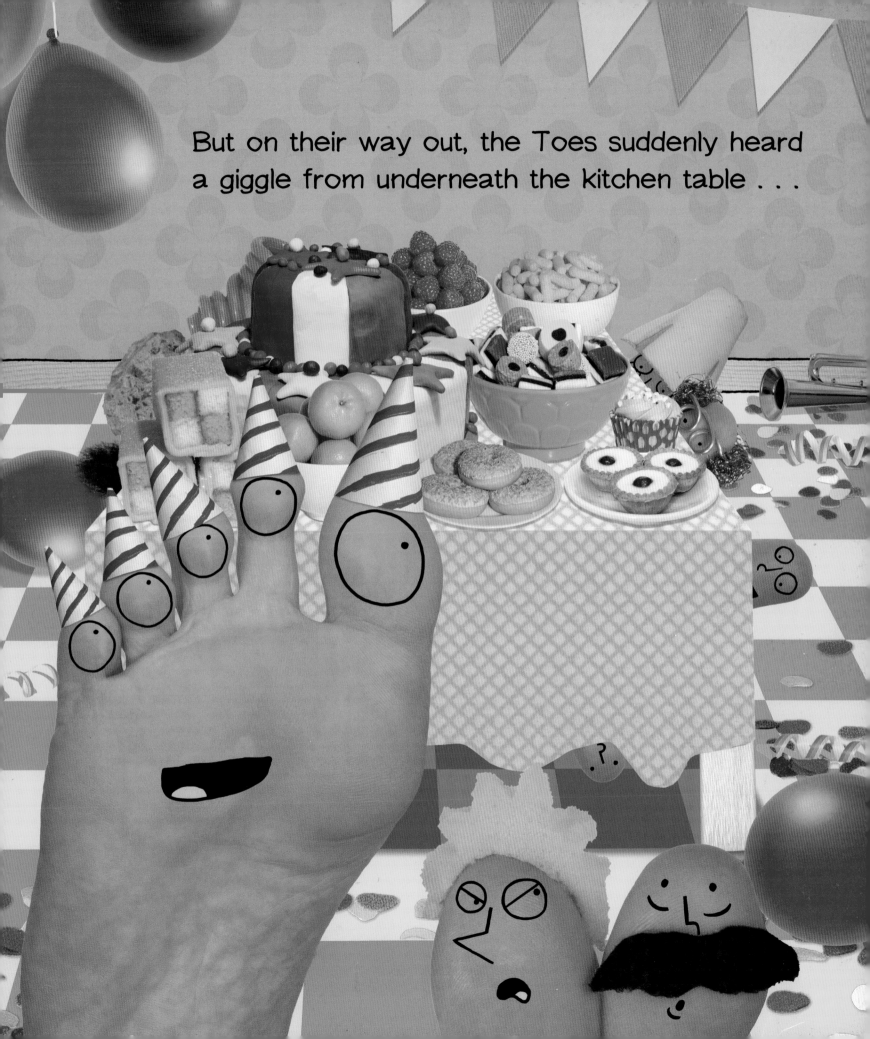

"We're so pleased you came to join the fun," said Finn, putting party hats on the Toes.

"NO! There's been a mistake!" Mrs Toe said, trying to rush to the door.

Everyone was dancing around them –
the Terrible Toes couldn't get out!

"Stop this party!" Mr Toe begged.
"Everyone please
STOP having fun!"

But the party was just getting started, and the Terrible Toes were stuck in the middle of it . . .

. . . for the rest of the night!
Ha ha, hee hee, ho ho!

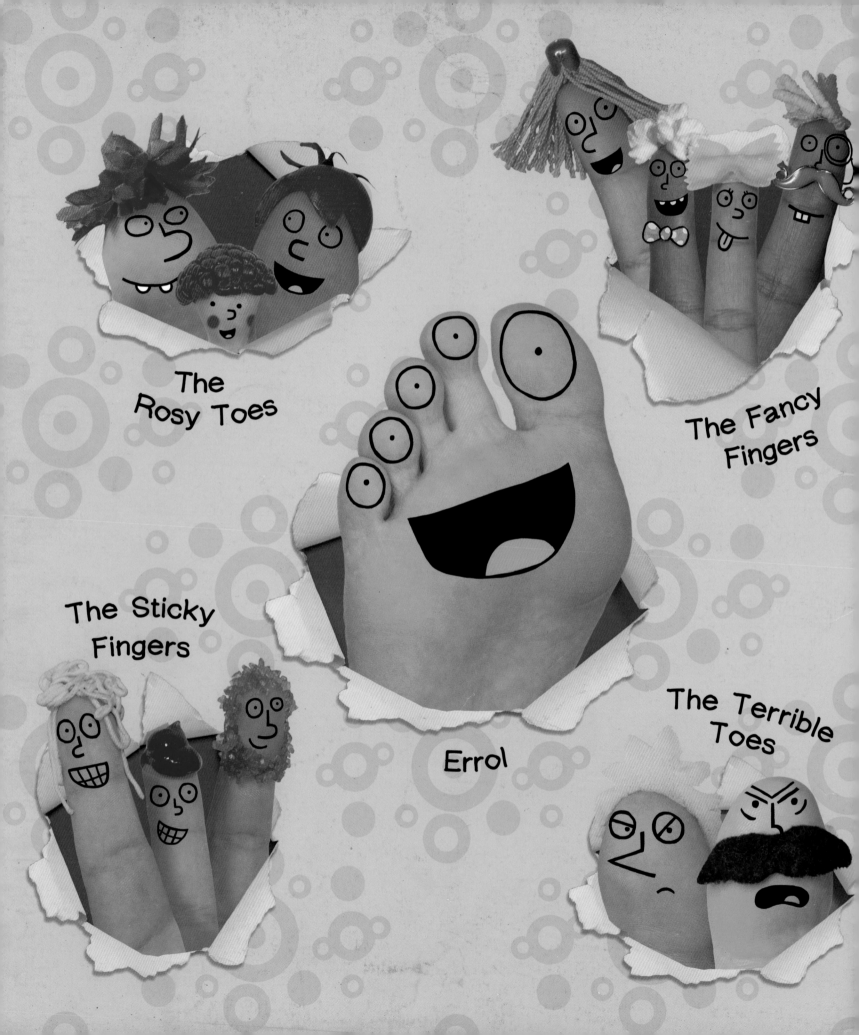

The
Rosy Toes

The Fancy
Fingers

The Sticky
Fingers

Errol

The Terrible
Toes